DALE

A Remarkable Woman's Quest For Love and Trust

by Robert Proctor

DORRANCE PUBLISHING CO
EST. 1920
PITTSBURGH, PENNSYLVANIA 15238

Dorrance Publishing Co
585 Alpha Drive
Pittsburgh, PA 15238
Visit our website at *www.dorrancebookstore.com*

ISBN: 979-8-8881-2456-7
eISBN: 979-8-8881-2956-2

Chapter One

Bogie had been cheating on her all along.

Dale's first inkling came when she was doing a load of wash and found a jeweler's receipt for ring adjustment in his pants pocket. It was dated five weeks before.

Suspicion was not part of Dale's nature though, so she merely wondered why Bogie would have such work done, especially when neither of them wore a ring. That evening she asked.

"Baby, what ring did you have adjusted?"

"What! What the hell you talkin' about? You been going through my personal stuff?"

Bogie's anger startled Dale. It seemed way out of proportion.

"I was just doing a load of wash, clearing out the pockets," she said. "I found this receipt from Sterling Jewelers."

Bogie exploded, "Don't you go looking through my private stuff!"

In their nine years together, they'd shared everything they had, everything they did. There was very little between them that was private. Or so it seemed.

Bogie turned and stormed out of the apartment, leaving Dale ruffled and confused. As he got in his car, Dale called to him, "Baby where you going? When you coming back?"

"Never mind!" Bogie yelled as he shoved his car into drive and screeched out of the parking lot.

It was a jarring look at her boyfriend. She'd never seen him like this, and she was left to wonder how a jeweler's receipt could provoke him so. After two hours, she called his cell. It went to voicemail. Two subsequent tries gave the same result.

She sat alone in the apartment that night. It was beginning to look like Bogie wasn't coming back. The TV was little more than a talking lamp as she sorted through the afternoon's blowup and Bogie's abrupt departure.

She needed a friend right then, someone to talk to. She thought of Eleanor, whom she was tight with back when they worked together at NatureSource Energy. Once Eleanor retired, they saw less of each other but had kept in touch. Dale called.

"Ellie, give me a call when you can," she said into the voicemail. "I've got some things going on."

Dale expected a fast call-back; Eleanor rarely was far from her phone. But no call came. This was one of those rare times.

Dale felt her options falling away. She was sinking into a deep loneliness. She just *had* to talk to somebody, vent, confide in somebody. Outside of Eleanor, the only other somebody who might give solace was Susan, whom she'd met and befriended during a political campaign some years before.

Maybe Susan feels like talking, Dale said to herself. *Not that I know what the hell I'm gonna tell her.*

Dale's call found Susan in the midst of coitus. Her words came out in breathless grunts as seemingly she'd answered her phone while having sex and never so much as paused when she took the call.

"Tell you what, Susan, I'll get back to you later," Dale said brusquely as she pressed the red circle on her phone. "We don't take calls while we're getting laid," she muttered.

Dale was put off by Susan's casual disregard for intimacy.

But intimacy of any kind was distinctly missing from Dale's life right now, and she felt it keenly. She sat on her couch in bra and panties, her go-to attire when she knew she'd be alone for a while. The scanty garb was a reliable way to put herself in touch with her body, the strikingly formed breasts and rump that gave her door-opening power with men. She felt strong in her near nakedness, in control, confident.   But her inner strength was being tested by the forces of this moment. She felt the painful tug of abandonment also at work in her.

To a large extent, Dale's body had defined her life to that point, for better and for worse. She had allowed men to experience her charms and sexual prowess for long periods, only to see the link dissolve when she found they'd cheated on her. It seemed to have happened again. Bogie was gone and might not be coming back. That jeweler's receipt was looking more and more like cheating. She was feeling lost and dispossessed. In time, she grew tearful.

An hour passed as Dale's emotions continued to churn. She felt an unbidden wave of desire coming over her. That confused her. The sounds of Susan about to climax in her bed, coupled with the looming absence of anything like that for her, had oddly stirred a longing for intimacy.

Dale tilted her head back and gazed at the ceiling. She let her legs part and slid her hand between them. She began stroking herself expertly. A familiar pleasure pulsed through her as she prodded. Fingers moving in slow circles produced a copious flow of moisture, staining the couch pillows. Dale paid it no heed. She soon was in the grip of frenzy. Her wild mix of emotions from the Bogie blowup were somehow fueling her sexual urges. She felt abruptly free of social restraints. She was alone in the room with naked lust.

She got up and lurched to the kitchen, reaching for a cucumber from the fridge. She urgently wanted it inside her. Arching her back over the marble countertop, Dale began to pull the chilled cucumber into her. Then she paused.

"No," she said aloud, "I want him on me."

She scuttled back to the couch, vegetable in hand, groaning under the weight of her lust. "Oooh, Oooh, Oooh!"

She fell back onto the couch, draping a leg onto the carpet. The panties were still on the kitchen floor. She wielded the cuke once more and with six firm nudges, she fully took it in. Her strokes were forceful, almost violent. Her legs and buttocks recoiled with each thrust. Her rapturous yells seemed to be coming from someone else. Through it all she tried to imagine Bogie mounted on top of her but her mind would not hold that image.

The orgasm hit her like crashing surf. Dale had never felt such intensity. When it finally subsided, she was sprawled on the couch, heaving for breath, a leg propped upright on the couch, the other splayed on the floor.

Dale had made a sodden mess of her couch, but upholstery cleaning would have to wait. Her funk was gone. She felt immense relief. The empty apartment now resonated with her chirps.

"Who needs Bogie!" she yelped.

It was the first spiteful thing she'd said about her missing boyfriend. She knew that veggies from the fridge were not a long-term fix for her problems, but she was glad for relief just the same.

Still wearing only her bra, Dale padded back into the kitchen clutching the glistening cucumber. She stood at the counter, pudenda giving their last drips. She knew she looked just as alluring as men had so often told her. If only she could find one who would be true.

She went after the cucumber. She peeled off the skin and sliced the fleshy fruit into a bowl. She popped a slice in her mouth, chewing slowly, deliberately as if performing a ritual. She popped another slice and ate, till she'd consumed half. She was about to cover the bowl and put it in the fridge, but she stopped. She picked out the remaining slices and dropped them one by one into the trash can.

With each slice that fell, she proclaimed loudly, "I'm done with phony turn-ons. I'm done with sham sex. I'm done with cheating men. I'm done with regret. I'm done with suffering. I'm done with sleeping alone. I'm done with all that."

As she let the can's lid fall with a sharp clank, a wry smile came to her face as she affirmed her resolution. Going forward, she would take charge of her intimate relations. She would do whatever she must to make them enjoyable and fulfilling. And honest.

She thought about it awhile, envisioned the cucumber she'd used for sex, then sliced up, partially devoured, and finally tossed aside. She saw it as a symbol of her pain, the torment of her shattered relationships. She felt like she'd wiped it out of her life.

Her tension drained away. A fresh smile wreathed her face. She felt light-hearted, even whimsical. She decided she'd call these new life vows her Cucumber Resolution.

· · · · · · · · ·

The resolution was going to need some time. She spent the night alone, got up next morning at the usual time and drove to work after a cursory breakfast of tea and toast. She was no longer exultant. She was sad at the state of affairs with Bogie—and still more than a little confused.

Days passed and Bogie never called. Then one day while Dale was at work, he let himself into her apartment and took out the clothes and belongings he'd kept there almost as a second home. As he departed for the last time, he left the door key on the table by the door.

After nine years of sharing life with Dale, all the while romping in bed like newlyweds, Bogie had, without a word, simply left her.

. . . .

As weeks gave way to months, Dale moved through her familiar routines as if by rote. Get up, go to work, come home, go to bed. Repeat as needed.

As she followed this dreary regimen, she longed for the life she vowed to make for herself right after Bogie left her. Her resolution was still out there to be realized.

But she needed more time. She was grappling with emotions that had not been resolved. Bogie had said nothing to her, so she wasn't able to focus her feelings. Anger, resentment, confusion, sympathy, relief—all took turns commanding her emotions. She feared at times that she might be coming apart.

She spoke frequently with her daughter, Gabrielle, who lived nearby with a friend. Gabby had always been close to her mother and now she saw the turmoil bedeviling Dale. She suggested moving in with her to help her through the crisis.

Dale immediately embraced the idea. She privately wondered why she hadn't thought of it first. Now she not only would have company again—it would be her beloved daughter.

Gabby made the move with ease, as nineteen-year-olds will do. No adjustment period was needed since Gabby had only been out on her own a little more than a year. Dale began to feel closer to normal. If only she could know why Bogie had left her.

. . . .

One day while she was putting in the workday at NatureSource, Dale's cellphone chimed. This was unusual, getting a call on her personal phone. She didn't recognize the caller's number, but she picked up on the third ring.

"Hello Dale, my name is Kristine, Kristine Blackman," an unfamiliar voice said. "I don't think you know me, but I have something important to tell you."

Dale just listened as Kristine spoke, haltingly at first.

"I'm calling to let you know what happened with Bogart," she said. "We have been together two years."

A chill came over Dale. She sensed her life was changing.

"I understand how this must sound to you," Kristine went on, "and I am truly sorry. You may take that for what it's worth."

As she listened, Dale sensed this call was equal measures of courtesy and smugness on Kristine's part. She wondered about this woman, where she came from, what she looked like.

Kristine continued, "Bogart and I will be getting married."

The words took a shattering toll. Dale struggled to breathe. Her hands and arms moved over her desk without purpose. She picked up a pencil, then dashed it on her appointment book. It all seemed so unreal to her. Unfocused thoughts darted through her head.

What were we doing two years ago? she wondered. Memories of concerts, picnics, days at the beach came and went in a blur. And the sex! Their sex life had been vigorously active the whole time. She knew she had satisfied Bogie in bed. She would know if he was ever losing interest but in plain fact, he never was. Dale had thoughts of Bogie showing up at Dale's place fresh from copulating with this other woman. Her tortured reflections didn't last long.

"Right now, I'm nine weeks pregnant," Kristine said.

Dale took in the words but had no feelings left to hurt.

"I called you because you need to know this. I told Bogart again and again to call you but he simply would not. I was very angry with him for that. I'm sorry to be the one bringing such unwelcome news to you. I regret that my happiness with Bogart is coming at your expense."

Dale noticed an edge coming into the woman's voice.

"But life is a game," she continued, "with winners and losers. When you lose, you have to learn to move on. That's just the way it is. Goodbye Dale."

Disjointed thoughts swirled in Dale's head. *Who is this woman and how did she meet Bogie?* she wondered. She also thought it likely that Kristine had romped with Bogie in the same bed he'd shared with Dale at his apartment. But just as upsetting was her spiteful "you have to learn to move on" remark. It struck Dale as ill-concealed crowing. She was offended and deeply hurt.

She realized she knew nothing about this woman who'd just upended her life with a phone call. Young or old? White or Black? Tall or short? She couldn't be sure from the brief phone call. The unknowns mounted with every thought that came to her. There was so much she didn't know, and likely would never know. She had to make herself stop wondering.

But the wounds opened by Kristine's call would not soon heal. Many still festered in her, especially the part about learning to move on when you lose. And she could not get over the reality that somewhere nearby an unborn child was developing, a child fathered by her recent lover.

Chapter Two

In all, it took Dale a few months to overcome her shock at the Bogie revelations. She busied herself with a daily routine that called for nine hours or more at the office.

Over her sixteen years working at NatureSource, Dale had been friendly toward her co-workers as they came and went with relatively brief careers there. But she had shared little about her personal affairs. Now, slowly she began to take small but deliberate steps toward getting to know them better, even though some had been working with her for years.

One morning at the coffee table near Dale's office, Marvin Byrne, a co-worker, was in the midst of a tirade, which seemed unusual for a setting with others milling about.

Dale pulled up a chair by the urn, folded her hands on her lap, and listened passively to Marvin's rant. It was a chance to get to know another worker. She knew him only as Marvin. The others were filing back to their desks with their coffee, and soon the two of them were virtually alone there. She was an audience of one.

Marvin saw his audience departing but he was in mid-rant and didn't want to stop. He was detailing the agonies of a man suddenly deprived of his fiancée.

"The least they could've done was give a little notice," he complained, "but they were like, 'Pack your bags, you're leaving Thursday.' Five weeks!" Marvin's thick shock of reddish-brown hair shuddered with his outburst.

The woman had been tabbed on scant notice by her sales manager for five weeks of business travel to promote a fast-growing line of human hair wigs that she co-founded, setting up franchises around the country.

"She hired the guy and now *he's* telling *her* where she's gotta go for new business—and when," Marvin grumbled.

The sudden departure left Marvin to tend their nest alone. He voiced little doubt about what he missed the most. He couldn't resist ill-disguised hints about his state of sexual "back-up".

Given her recent history, Dale had little pity for the man's personal plight. Sensing that nobody else would hear them, she finally offered, "Marvin, surely it can't be that hard for a man like you to find somebody to hump."

Marvin was stunned by the sudden candor.

"All you need to do is find a woman," she added. "Just about any woman will do it for you."

Regaining his bearings, Marvin thought about Dale's bold double *entendre*. He played along.

"But where do you find a woman who actually *will* do it for me?" he wondered aloud.

Dale had anticipated the question, even knowing the man would not be seriously thinking of cheating on his fiancée.

She saw the thundering irony in that thought.

Plainly, the task of finding a woman on short notice would be Marvin's problem alone, but there's no shortage of willing women in this world.

"I mean I could go home with you right now and hump you till you begged me to stop."

The world stopped turning. All humanity stood and stared at Dale in disbelief for what she had just said. Dale was gob smacked by her words! How could they come out so wrong? Such an unseemly lapse with her co-worker right there in the office. She'd all but offered to do something she wouldn't ever do as long as she lived. And she never saw it coming.

To Dale's thinking, it was one thing to talk plainly about someone's problems, even their intimate ones. But to offer up her own self that way? It was simply not how Dale Burton conducted herself. Her new openness with co-workers surely never intended anything like *this*! She flushed hot with humiliation.

Marvin, barely able to speak after this unexpected frankness, finally managed to say, "Would you really *do* that?"

This was Dale's get-out-of-jail-free card! She had merely to say she was only kidding in order to make a point. Her inner voice was screaming, *just say it!* But the words would not come out. She started several times to offer a better version, only to feel it melt away as something she didn't really mean. She didn't want to come across as hardhearted or uncaring.

And this. As she saw it, the nature of Marvin's reaction made her want to keep the fantasy going a bit longer. He was embarrassed too, and she could feel it. They had become partners in embarrassment. There would still be time to say she didn't mean it literally, she decided. At the same time, Dale felt a startling appeal to being any kind of partner again, even in her own thoughts. Suddenly there were so many things to think about.

"I would be willing to do that for you, Marvin... sure... to help you in your time of trial," she offered, trying gamely to add some lightness.

But Marvin's discomfort had vanished like steam on a hot stove. So had any thought of his fiancée. He was already sold on the idea.

"Well, why don't we just get out of here right now and go straight to my place?" he blustered.

"Okay, let's," Dale heard herself saying, knowing she'd missed her last chance for a graceful exit. Untangling herself just got a lot harder.

But to her sudden surprise, she felt little regret for her rashness. She felt herself being tugged in another direction she had not counted on. She was actually starting to turn over thoughts of having sex... with Marvin, of all people.

It had been two years since she broke with Bogie in what started as a rebound relationship following her failed eight-year marriage. But the Bogie days went on for nine years marked by regular bouts of exuberant sex. Subtly but steadily, they escorted Dale most of the way through her prime years. Now, as she approached middle age, Dale found she'd missed some of the good things in life, many of which come with committed relationships, she believed.

She knew she missed the sex. She missed it on a physical level far more than she thought she would. And she'd long known that masturbation was at best a barren refuge, as the night of the cucumber had starkly reminded her.

In this moment, she became more keenly aware of what she'd been missing, the desires she'd been suppressing, the itch that now cried out to be scratched. It suddenly seemed the possibility of actual in-the-flesh sex excited her more than she expected or was willing to admit even to herself.

· · · · · · · ·

As Marvin drove the eight miles to his house with Dale, it was plain to see he was ill at ease. Dale wondered if the morning's events worried him. They worried *her*. She wanted badly to ask Marvin if he was sure about all this, but she felt it would make her look capricious and small.

I cannot believe this is real, she thought. *I'm not really on my way to Marvin's house to get laid. This just isn't happening.*

Unreal as it all seemed, there were other matters that were all too real. She tried to assure herself that nobody was witness to their exchange that morning that led them to bolt out of the office to parts unknown. She replayed their office encounter over and over in her head trying to recall if anybody had been near enough to listen in. She was all but certain nobody had. Neither had anyone witnessed the stunning out-of-body gaff that turned Dale's small talk into a scandalous proposition. And probably nobody noticed them leaving together in his car. She had to replay the whole scene a few times over before she could be sure. And she still had no idea what made her propose humping Marvin.

It's not that she didn't find him attractive with his trim, athletic body and bold thatch of auburn hair. She did, just not in a way that even suggested intimacy. Working in an office setting, she could not allow herself to fancy a male colleague in a personal way—that could be a career-ender—and so she had not. Also, by timeless popular norms, Marvin had removed himself from the ranks of available males when he got engaged, and unmarried females like Dale made the necessary shift in their thoughts and desires.

What's more, as a Black woman, Dale had long known that interracial relations of *any* kind demanded special heed. The slightest glance or inference could be taken wrong and lead to jealousy, spite or worse. This was yet another barrier.

Then too there was the age gap. Marvin was young and about to be married. Dale was much older and had long since found marriage unworkable. She had been living quietly with Gabby since she split with her husband and, shortly after, took up with Bogie.

Most relationships take time and patience to build, especially when things like race and age pose tensions. But it seemed Dale and Marvin had come all the way in a few hours, propelled by the sheer force of her salacious remark that morning. It had set a definite tone for their activities to follow.

Despite all the factors working against them, they'd managed to skirt the critical steps of building a relationship, and move straight to sex.

Marvin pulled into the garage and lowered the garage door so's to thwart any nosey neighbors. He and Dale entered the well-appointed six room ranch through the kitchen.

As they stood amid counters, appliances and gleaming cookware hanging from hooks, an acute awkwardness fell on them. An hour ago, they were working through their morning business in the offices of NatureSource Energy, and now they were standing in Marvin's kitchen about to have sex.

Those two poles of their unfolding day could not have been more different. Routine had become wild; casual had become intense; associates had become intimates. From a moment's conversation, the fabric of their lives had changed fundamentally. They couldn't get that out of their minds.

Marvin was privately worried they may have been seen by neighbors as they pulled into the driveway. What a sight they would have been, he thought. It was well known by all who would listen that Marvin was living alone for five weeks while Shannon Pierce, his fiancée, was away on business. Now here he was showing up at the house with a stranger, a full-figured Black woman who was manifestly not Shannon.

Dale felt the awkwardness too.

Marvin turned to her and muttered half-heartedly, "Something to drink?"

"Oh no... no thanks," Dale replied distractedly. They didn't come here for iced tea and small talk, and they both knew it.

Finally, the urgency that had grown in Marvin since Dale made her shocking offer became too much for him.

"I think it's time to go to another room," he murmured. "Come with me." He strode head-down toward the room at the far end of the hallway where the corner of a bed was visible through the open door.

Dale followed, recognizing things for what they were. The time had come. She was committed to performing sexually. She knew the rules would be different once she entered that bedroom. Any kind of touching would no longer be discouraged as it would back at Eversource, or anywhere else in society. In fact, touching would be the order of the day.

But even now the outlandish nature of their situation still hounded Dale. She knew she was taking a big chance, slipping away from work with a fellow employee whom she knew only as a colleague, proposing to have sex with him, trusting to his discretion. She was going to get to know this co-worker a whole lot better, to say the least, and she wondered where that would lead. What would their lives be like after today?

Obsessive thinking would not go away.

Marvin closed the bedroom door as if to mark the official start of their afternoon together. Dale glimpsed herself in the mirror on the door. She was well turned out in black dress and coordinated grey jacket. That was about to change.

Scrolling through her thoughts as she lay down her jacket and pulled off her shoes, Dale took comfort in knowing her new sex partner was likely free of any STDs since he'd been dutifully devoted to his fiancée these last few years. Until today, that is.

"Marvin, you don't have any, uh, infections or anything, do you?"

"No, of course not. I'd have said something." Then he added, "What about you Dale?"

Dale was tempted to mention her extended celibacy and how sexually transmitted disease gets transmitted, yes, mostly through sex. She also thought of mentioning her age. But all that would've called for more snark than she was ready for just then.

"No, I'm fine, Marvin," she said.

Then Marvin said one more thing. "This wouldn't be a good time to get pregnant either."

Dale was unexpectedly touched by the mention of pregnancy. She'd stopped using birth control when she broke up with Bogie. It made perfect sense. Her sex life had come to an abrupt halt with the break-up. Now, a couple of years later, she was forty-three, and even though she still had her monthly periods, cramps and all, she knew pregnancy was a long shot. She thought it a little crude of Marvin to bring it up, but she found the notion exciting nonetheless.

Marvin was not of a mind to deliberate such matters. He would leave those niceties to Dale's good judgment. He was on a roll today, he figured, and luck was on his side. Feverish lust had overtaken him. He was pulling off his shirt with reckless haste, popping buttons as he pulled. Dale felt his hectic pace and didn't like it.

"Slow down mister," she said to him.

Marvin hesitated but only for a moment. Dale pulled the cord to adjust the blinds on the window, which looked out on the lawn and an evergreen hedge. The mid-day glare faded from the room.

"That's a little better," she said softly.

Pulling the blinds actually made things a *lot* better. It helped Dale see not just the room in a different light, but her whole afternoon. Everything looked a lot more inviting now. In essence, she wanted more than merely to hump Marvin in the bright light of day just to prove a point about "willing women". She wanted in on the excitement.

She at last became consciously aware of the resolution. She wanted their tryst to be pleasurable for both of them. But Dale's intuition told her that if mutual satisfaction was going to happen, she would have to make it happen. She would have to call the shots.

Dale's thoughts were at war with each other. One part of her was preparing for the alien experience of sex with a man she knew only by his first name. She knew she was taking risks with no guarantee of reward. Her reputation, her job, even her self-respect stood to be compromised if this liaison went badly.

The "humping" compact they'd so casually made in the office called for little more than Dale spreading her legs for Marvin just as long as he pleased. And nothing more.

Another part of her saw the possibilities for intense pleasure in spreading those legs. Yes, she admitted, their compact was one-sided and crude, but it had promise. It would be up to Dale to take her full measure of enjoyment.

Dale also was darkly aware that she was helping Marvin be unfaithful to Shannon, and in effect she was acting out the sins that had killed her last two relationships. She struggled with the poisonous potential of it.

But the rituals of sex have their own rules, and morality at times is little more than a timid advisor in the presence of lust.

Truth was, when it came to carnal matters, Dale knew the score. She knew the sexual pleasure she could deliver; and she knew it was far greater than Shannon Pierce could ever begin to match. She simply knew. She also knew that when problems developed for the young couple she, Dale Burton, would be the "other woman" who caused it.

Memories flashed in Dale's head of the gripping moments when she found her mates had cheated. The sudden, wrenching emptiness when a bond of loving trust is blown to pieces.

Today's events had the same possibilities for the young couple, Dale knew. That was the bald reality of this moment, and her abrupt awareness of it hit her like a fist.

Dale fought to settle her warring thoughts. She saw disaster waiting if she waded into a sexual encounter feeling any guilt. Sex was still the main event this afternoon. And it was she, after all, who'd started this whole affair with her unguarded blurt. To further complicate things, Dale knew she first had to take the edge off Marvin's raging lust. But she didn't want to be abrupt about it.

A little tease might set a more agreeable tone, Dale decided. While examining a pair of Jeff Koons posters on the wall, she declared, "Oh, I really like these exhibition prints. Do you have any others?"

Not waiting for an answer that would never come, she unsnapped her dress behind her neck and let it slide to the floor. A black dress lying on the floor can be a powerful symbol. Dale understood the power. She glanced down at it in mock surprise.

"Oops!" she chirped as though it had slipped off by accident.

Dale's good looks had often made her the center of attention. Since her early teens she'd been the most attractive person in the room. She was used to being looked at, admired, and she had unconsciously taken to striking poses wherever she was.

Great as Dale looked in clothes, she grew even more arresting as they came off. Men had found her lavish thighs hypnotically inviting. She arranged herself on the bed, clad only in panties, bra and lace-trimmed camisole. She had worn no hose that day; she seldom did. Her coffee hued legs lay elegantly over the powder blue bedspread. They made a symphony of colors and shapes.

She slipped the camisole over her head and let it fall where it may. Marvin was still grunting and tugging furiously at his trousers, finally flinging them aside. He was wearing only his socks—which in his rush he'd neglected to take off—and his boxers. Dale could see he was already aroused.

She knew her next move would be defining. Speaking not a word, she pulled her bra around so the closure was in front where she could see it. Her mountainous breasts tumbled over the bra strap before she could actually remove it. But when she did pull it away and toss it onto a chair she was fully displaying the same legendary breasts that for years had sent men in the office into rapturous fantasies.

Boldly filling out her torso from breast bone to tummy, Dale's bosom commanded the room. In fact, Dale's body was of a type that defies the burglaries of age. The four pounds she'd put on since her twenties had gathered agreeably around her thighs and rump, only enhancing their fullness to men's appraising eyes. She had taken good care of herself over the years. She ate sensibly and even managed to work out with weights now and then to stay toned and keep the bulges in the right places.

But Dale's extraordinary energies, good looks, and bodily assets were natural to her. She was a modern wonder.

She had maintained a modest and demure public persona. Her choice in clothing was fashionable and tasteful, and not notably revealing. She never flaunted her assets. She knew that men universally coveted her transcendent breasts but she had a withering glare for any who simply gaped at them. And talking about them within her earshot was similarly taboo.

But she also knew the bedroom was a place to let her inner feelings show, and at this moment her anticipation was swelling. Wearing only her panties now, Dale sat on the bed and took matters in hand.

"Hmmmm," she purred as she grasped the waistband on Marvin's shorts."

He tried to speak but only choked.

Dale gave the shorts a quick tug and let them drop, puddling at his feet. Marvin stepped out of them and stood, rampantly erect, facing her. Dale averted her eyes and beamed confidently into Marvin's face.

Her pulse was pounding now. This was her moment of truth, her chance to gauge the actual size and heft of the organ she was about to bring into her life. No more guessing what's inside the shorts. But she was approaching the moment with due ceremony. She would not gawk like a teenager, she decided. She would take her first look discretely.

Certainly Dale was no stranger to male anatomy. A woman of her charms would have more than a few suitors in her time, and it was for Dale to choose prudently among them. This she did. Still, over the years she had seen her share of naked men, and she thought she was beyond surprising.

She let her eyes fall to Marvin's crotch.

What she saw caused her no little arousal. To Dale's eyes Marvin's "package" was like an eight-inch wiejska sausage coursing with veins. It seemed alive to her. It was wreathed by a short, curly growth of his signature russet hair. Dale had seen no others like it.

On the one hand she delighted in knowing she still could arouse a man so abundantly. On the other, she shuddered as she thought of that much girth actually inside her.

Will it hurt? she wondered. *Will I bleed? Will it even fit inside me?* Despite these worries, Dale was thrilled by Marvin's penis.

As for Marvin, he had to wonder what would come next; Dale had called the shots to this point. His answer came quickly. She pulled him onto the bed and turned him on his back. She pushed his legs apart adroitly and crawled between them, reaching for him as she rose to her knees, and taking him deep into her throat.

Dale knew this was going to be a brief performance; Marvin was palpably ready to ejaculate. She had seen it building in him. And now she felt it.

She had planned his sexual response for the afternoon and now she was making it happen.

Marvin shrieked and convulsed at the first spasm as if electrified. Dale drew away deftly, strands of spittle festooning from her mouth. Marvin's ejaculate splatted on his face, chest and belly, as well as the powder blue bedspread. Dale managed to dodge the pearly spurts even while keeping her grip on him. She finished him off with smooth, firm strokes and left him limp on the bed, arms splaying, head lolling.

Dale had never seen the life go out of a man so completely.

The job had taken less than a minute, such was Marvin's urgency. Dale saw it as a necessary first step. She knew Marvin in his agitation was little more than a ticking bomb and needed to be partially "disarmed" before she could even think about copulating with him. She had her *own* pleasure to see about.

Dale was beginning to assemble her new laws of intimacy and fulfillment.

She knew Marvin would recover quickly. The humping was still to come. Dale knew if she were to feel satisfaction in this afternoon's liaison, humping would still be the primal force that got it started.

But her new desires had begun working from the moment she entered this unfamiliar bedroom. Dale understood the many ways a man and woman can enjoy each other to the fullest. And she knew more than ever that she wanted to be a willing, vigorous participant.

After a few minutes sitting on the bed feathering her fingers over Marvin's legs, she decided her new partner was ready for the next step.

She stood up and reached for her panties. Gliding them down her shapely legs and kicking them aside, she noticed Marvin beginning to swell again as she went nude.

"Now Marvin," she said, "we've got some humping to do."

She knew her use of "humping" would spark even greater lust in him. Dale had seen the word's almost magic effect on Marvin when she first spoke it in the office. It had an unmistakable naughtiness to it even while calling up images of vigorous, mindless coitus.

In fact, at the office just hours before, that very mindset had led her to tell Marvin how easily he could take care of his sexual urges. Right there, Dale had set the tone for carnal adventure to follow. She had even set the only limit: "Till you begged me to stop."

Marvin, as expected, was again fully aroused. Once more Dale moved on him.

"Lie back please," she whispered.

She faced him on the bed and squatted gracefully like a dark sumo rikishi, lowering herself onto him. This was it! This was the precise moment she'd envisioned when she first glimpsed Marvin's erection, and now she was about to take it into her body. She paused, reaching down to grasp him and assure a proper entry.

As she reopened herself to sex for the first time in years, Dale's thoughts darted again and again to how far she'd come since morning, and the matter-of-fact, almost impersonal way she'd offered her body as a thing, a receptacle for this sex-deprived man.

She had indeed come a long way.

Dale also was feeling the strong hormonal effects of their encounter now, and she indulged her new feelings. Her breath came in wheezes. Sweat glistened on her body. She was consummately turned on.

She continued lowering onto Marvin, slowly, till he gave a long soulful moan at the deep penetration. Dale for her part let out breath with a kind of whimper, then another, as she sat astride Marvin, getting used to the size of him inside her, humping him slowly at first, now faster, just as she'd promised.

Their climax came with harmonic precision. In truth, Dale felt it back-to-back, the second time more urgently than the first.

She lay there, spent, yet quietly jubilant at her sexual capacities. Marvin had entered a dreamlike state in which unimaginably good things just kept getting better. He closed his eyes for long moments, taking in the bliss.

They were having a very productive workday.

Lying there awhile, they hardly spoke but both understood more sex lay ahead in their self-declared marathon. Steadily they regathered themselves, lust seeping back into their loins till they were both again ready for each other.

Suddenly, impulsively, Marvin seized the initiative. He reached for Dale and flopped her over on her belly. She responded at once, rising to her knees as he grasped her hips from behind. They were moving in bed like two accomplished wrestlers on a mat.

He entered her again, his hands straying from her hips to her breasts which hung pendulously down to the sheets.

Dale, on hands and knees, canted her head and whispered urgently, "Hump me, Marvin, hump me!"

Marvin needed no prodding. He steadied himself now and deepened his thrusts. Dale rose to the moment as intense shudders again ran through her body. Her breathing quickened and grew labored as the orgasm enveloped her, consumed her, released her.

As they uncoupled, Dale fell face-down on the bed and let out a long breath. Marvin reached for her and gently rolled her over as her legs parted. The man could not resist this inviting pose. Hardly pausing, he positioned himself between her legs and braced himself on his arms.

Dale was physically sapped, and awash in the fluids of sex, but she gamely lifted her legs and pulled him to her, wringing out his very last measure of lust.

In all, the humping went on—in one form or another—till the afternoon shadows were growing long in the bedroom. They'd been at it more than four hours.

By mutual arrangement, these two office colleagues had just given themselves over to a strenuous afternoon of sex. It was such a bizarre departure for them. And even though they had done exactly what they came for, they struggled to comprehend it. They lay together unspeaking, overwhelmed by turbulent feelings.

Their workday morning had started routinely, and casual conversation had in a moment's flash escalated into a life-altering afternoon.

It occurred to Marvin that this undreamed-of adventure with his co-worker had happened in the very bed he regularly slept in with Shannon.

He was also aware that Dale, in the years he'd known her, had spoken very little about her personal life, preferring to listen to the stories of others. And yet this woman not only had given him a willing reception for his misplaced loneliness, she'd also led him through a sexual trek unlike any he'd ever had—or ever *would* have.

She was nearly twenty years his senior, yet her smooth and ample flesh, her poise and comely features had enthralled him, rousing him again and again to ultimate satisfaction. He knew he could not pretend this afternoon had never happened.

They lay together, inert, in stark contrast to the hours they'd just shared.

Dale reflected on how the sex she'd spoken about so off-handedly that morning had just given her electric pleasures she'd only dreamed of in recent years. She had once again felt the urgent pulsations of a man inside her. My, how she had missed that, she thought.

Truth be told, the thrusts Marvin had given her with his astonishing member, were far more rousing than she possibly could have expected. She felt more sensually awake than ever in her life.

All the same, Dale was glad she'd left off with Marvin when she did. She knew neither of them had anything left to give. She realized, fleetingly, that she'd not made Marvin "beg her to stop" as she'd rashly foretold. Such crowing had no relevance now. She absolutely did not care. She was sure Marvin didn't either.

They would of course need to shower. Dale wondered how that would go, their bodies together again. It went according to a timeless, unspoken plan.

They followed their natural impulse to gently lather-up each other's bodies while the warm water sluiced down on them. Marvin made sure that all of Dale's breathtaking bosom was well and wholly lathered, and also fondled, squeezed, and gently kissed.

Dale, for her part, turned to Marvin's own sexual apparatus. As she held it in her hand, she recalled the intensity of it upon first entering her body. She squeezed the prodigious loaf to mark the moment.

They stood face to face in the steam and pulsing water, letting their unhurried hands perform this ritual. Then, responding to an inner cue, they both recognized it was time to let go. Their satisfaction was complete.

It was as close to perfect as Dale could ever hope for in such strange circumstances. She felt a wakening spirit begin to rise in her. Her resolution was starting to bear fruit.

Moments later, as Dale primped her hair in the mirror, she had an impish desire to go back one last time to her original brashness about sex.

"You see how simple it is, Marvin?" she cooed playfully. "It's just a matter of finding somebody to hump."

Dale now realized, to her new delight, the same applied just as well to her.

CHAPTER THREE

On day two of the resolution, Dale slept late, called in sick, and tried over several cups of tea to feel better about things.

It was as if the Dale who drove home Wednesday evening was trying to rearrange the furniture in her head, and the Dale who'd gone to work that morning wasn't having it. The only true reality was her sore and bruised body, a tender memento of adults colliding repeatedly in energetic sex.

Finally, after mulling the disjointed questions, recollections, doubts and fears swirling in her head, she realized she simply had to have more information.

She wanted to call Marvin to talk about so much of it, yet she knew the risks in that. They were enormous. Marvin might be the same as ever, she mused, unaffected by yesterday's wild events. Dale doubted it. She knew she'd left her mark on him. The real question was, what would he do about it?

Calling him, especially now, would be a snake pit of complications. But she did need to know some basics. She felt safe in assuming Marvin wanted their tryst to forever be a secret. She thought up alibis for their whereabouts that Wednesday afternoon. She and Marvin would have to agree on the particulars and live by them.

What's it going to be like at work? she wondered. *How will we interact? Like nothing ever happened?*

Of course! It had to be like that, like nothing happened, Dale decided. There was no getting around it. They had to be disciplined about it.

Still, Dale wondered if the sight of Marvin would trigger any kind of feelings in her. That was very much an unknown.

Would she feel revulsion for his improbity toward his fiancée? Doubtful, especially since Dale was the one who started the whole thing with her humping comment.

Would she feel sexually attracted? She couldn't rule that out even though, before yesterday, she'd had no feelings at all toward Marvin.

Nevertheless, the primal clarity of their sexual union could not be denied. By nearly any physical measure, the sex had been great. Dale also knew it could be a one-and-done. In fact, it had to be.

"It's absolutely game over," she decided. "The man has a fiancée. They have plans for the future. They have a house."

Indeed, they do have a house, Dale mused. She wasn't cynical by nature, but she couldn't set aside the reality that, yes, she'd had a chance to look at that house.

"That's the place where Marvin and Shannon will live," she said. "It's a fine suburban ranch, plenty of modern touches. The bathroom, for example, features a large walk-in shower with seats and rails and adjustable pulse shower head. I remember it well. I very much enjoyed the liberty I took there exploring Marvin's amazing genitals."

That was also the place where Marvin lathered soap on Dale's nipples and aroused them to a fine titillated rigidness.

"And the bedroom!" Dale went on. "How I reveled in their very excellent bed with its state-of-the-art mattress that stood up to the relentless pounding we gave it. Yes, and the lovely powder blue bedspread which Marvin now needs to take to the cleaners."

Dale broke from her reverie and found herself still wondering what Marvin was thinking. She needed to talk to him privately, but she realized she didn't know his cell number. She didn't even know his full name! Calling his desk phone from the outside could be hugely awkward.

"Please connect me to Marvin. You know, the young guy in consumer relations." Dale thought of other ways to describe the man too, but she doubted the operator would take it well.

She didn't even know if he was at work today. Maybe he had reacted to yesterday's events the same way she had. Maybe he stayed home. That too could pose problems, she thought, since the two of them had disappeared from the office at the same time the day before.

The resolution was off to a rocky start.

Dale was gulping her third cup of tea and making an effort to focus on pleasant thoughts. Inevitably, she found herself counting off the high points of her four-hour sexual adventure. It was indeed a pleasurable time, she had to admit, even though it exhausted her.

It was born of embarrassment and bluster, executed with guile and secrecy, shrouded in guilt and distraction—but damn, it felt good!

Things were looking up. If epic sex were needed to spawn an awakening in Dale, a new appreciation of sensual pleasure, a new start to a life of reward and fulfillment, then she had met the requirement. Next would come new adventures with new men, new sex partners.

What are you thinking, girl! bellowed her inner voice.

The sudden thought of this new plan repelled her deeply. She saw that she'd gotten carried away in planning her personal renaissance entirely around sex.

It was, among other things, dramatically out of character. Dale's self-image demanded a modest demeanor for the world at large. Her sexual appetites were known only to a few and were for the bedroom only, she decided. She would never allow herself to be unchaste in pursuit of companionship.

Then her phone rang.

The world of here and now returned. Marvin was in a stew over the situation. He had all the same concerns that Dale had, and then some. His engagement to Shannon made things much dicier. He was distraught. He was also smitten. It became clear to Dale that Marvin had been overwhelmed by her adroit performance in bed. He craved more.

Well, that complicates things, Dale mused to herself. But she was not surprised by Marvin's sudden devotion; it was common for men who'd met her to be swept away by her charms.

They talked further but without much purpose. They did vow to keep their affair secret, come what may, but the future of their relationship remained up in the air.

Their lives were moving in different directions now. But for the small slice of time remaining to them, they could meet again somewhere, maybe for the last time. They needed to find a secret place. That is, any place where they could enjoy lengthy and unrestricted sex.

Safe to say they both were open to having sex again. Marvin wanted it desperately, irrationally. And Dale was willing to settle for a little more Marvin. But she could see that Marvin didn't want to end their trysts any time soon, even after his fiancée came home. She knew that could trigger much bigger problems all around.

As for their secret place, their sanctuary, Marvin's house was no longer an option; Shannon was due home in a few days. Dale and Marvin both knew the unspoken truth that sex—especially those sexual endurance runs they'd been having—leaves a trail of clues and traces that keep turning up.

Dale's apartment might serve the purpose, but it lacked privacy partly because Gabby had continued living with her mother after the divorce and for most of the Bogie period. But Dale feared more for her reputation if her gossipy neighbors could hear their bedroom thunder, and track Marvin's comings and goings.

She thought of her friends. Who among them could be trusted with a big secret? And who among them also had a spare bedroom? Her inventory of friends all seemed flawed in one small way or another when it came to meeting those needs.

Then she remembered Eleanor, her old friend. Over the years at NatureSource and after, they'd had long talks about life and confessed their peccadilloes to each other. Eleanor loved a good story, but when she was bound to secrecy her lips were tight. She was perfect. Dale wondered why she didn't think of Eleanor first.

She wanted to see if her friend was up for a little intrigue. She called.

Dale told Eleanor about the situation only in general terms, and then asked her bluntly if she would provide shelter and comfort to lovers who needed a place to meet. Even without details her meaning was clear enough.

Eleanor was hesitant. "Mind telling me why you're looking for a place where two lovers can meet?"

"Ellie, honey, one of the lovers is me."

Eleanor was shocked but thrilled that Dale finally had a man back in her life. Dale held back many of the basic facts about Marvin, letting Eleanor assume he was roughly Dale's age, and true love was the only driver. Eleanor would have to find out that Marvin was just a callow youth by comparison. As Dale saw it, Eleanor might then assume that Marvin was really just a stud service. She could live with that.

Dale called Marvin with word about their new arrangement. Marvin blubbered with excitement, heedless of his risks. And Dale found that she too was already looking forward to it. Pelvic twinges let her know.

CHAPTER FOUR

Eleanor's place was a rustic delight. It was a well-kept farmhouse sitting at the end of a long dirt road on the outskirts of town. It was surrounded on three sides by ungrazed pasture that stretched toward distant woodlands. To people looking for peace and privacy, Eleanor's house was paradise.

Dale arrived around three o'clock, well ahead of Marvin, and parked her Honda next to the porch. Eleanor, wearing denim overalls and her sandy–grey hair in a bun, had already come out to greet her. They hugged and began gabbing animatedly. Eventually Dale got around to the "tryst thing" which by now had truly sparked Eleanor's interest.

Dale knew her friend would not blanch as the details were revealed, Marvin's age, his domestic situation, his-coworker status. Indeed, Eleanor's grin grew wider with the telling. She remembered Marvin because his arrival at NatureSource came a few months before her retirement. The need for secrecy was painfully clear. She was thrilled to be a co-conspirator.

Dale had arrived early so she could be waiting in the spare bedroom when Marvin was brought there by Eleanor. It was Dale's little scheme to enhance the moment. Eleanor was only too happy to play the part of merry innkeeper, even though she also saw more than a few touches of gentle madam.

Marvin arrived fifteen minutes later, saw Dale's car, and parked next to it. Dale had told him she wanted to "catch up" with Eleanor awhile before he came, and that Marvin should just come in through the kitchen when he got there. Eleanor greeted him as he entered, introduced herself, and beckoned him to follow her to the guest bedroom. She gave him only the barest explanation and the suggestion that he remove his shoes. The drapes had been drawn to darken the bedroom.

Marvin closed the door behind him. He again was being led. He stepped warily forward. When his eyes adjusted to the darkness, he saw an object on the hardwood by his feet. He leaned over.

It was an enormous black brassiere. He picked it up, noticing Dale's body scent on it. Marvin felt his heartbeat tick upward. He had some idea what was up, but nothing for sure, except that Dale was likely very nearby. He looked toward the bed but couldn't make out detail. A few steps closer he saw another object on the floor.

It was a black pair of panties trimmed with lace. It had the heady fragrance of Dale's cosseted crotch, to which Marvin had grown immoderately devoted. He now was beside himself with lust.

Dale had slipped from the closet as he made his way to the bed holding Dale's undergarments. She came up behind him and placed her arms over his shoulders. Clasping her hands, she drew him into her nakedness.

Marvin was again in the position of having his pleasure dished out as Dale decided. He was getting used to it and he loved it. She ran her hands down over his chest and abdomen, stopping at his crotch. The bulge was bigger than ever. It seemed to Dale that her "enhanced moment" with Marvin was a success. Wishing to avoid the jumbled thrashing that Marvin displayed getting his pants off the day before, Dale slipped around in front of him and sat on the bed, expertly freeing him from his trousers. She had no trouble with his shorts either.

Marvin had managed to unbutton his shirt while Dale was doing her work. There he stood in his open shirt beside the bed. She took him into her mouth and could already feel Marvin's tremors beginning. It went much like their opening encounter the day before.

There was one difference: Marvin was standing and facing Dale. She was unperturbed by his gush. Anointed as she was, she did something she hadn't done in all of their last encounter. She kissed Marvin. She smothered his mouth with her plentiful lips and slipped her tongue inside.

Marvin was beyond excitement. Every move that Dale made was new territory for him. Her entire body seemed to pulse with intense current. In his life he'd never been with anyone as sexually gifted as Dale, even at her advanced age. He knew this as surely as he knew his name. Intuitively, he also knew he would never know such pleasure with anyone else as long as he lived. That very clearly included his planned life with Shannon.

While these thoughts churned ominously below the surface, Marvin was absorbed in the moment. Dale had laid on top of him, spreading her lustrous brown limbs over him. She pressed her body to his. Marvin reacted in his predictable way—by squirming, moaning, looking to the heavens, and getting stiff as hickory.

Dale mounted him. She moved her hips in slow, tiny thrusts to keep Marvin engaged. Marvin typically was racing through it all, but Dale meant to break that pace. She drew out her seductive moves over the passing minutes. Marvin was vaguely aware that he'd never stayed aroused this long before. Dale was putting him in touch with many new things.

After bringing Marvin to an almost intolerable level of physical desire, Dale let the dam burst. Her hips thrusted harder now, and Marvin's hair-trigger state went straight to climax. The sensation that washed through him was something he'd never felt before. Marvin bellowed in amazement. He grabbed a pillow and pressed it onto his face to muffle his outburst.

But if he intended to keep Eleanor from hearing them there, the pillow was not nearly enough. In fact, Eleanor was hearing everything as she chopped vegetables in the kitchen. She *wanted* to hear everything. She wanted to know how her friend Dale was faring. She was intrigued by their relationship. And most of all, Eleanor was indulging a cascade of her own lustful thoughts.

One lonesome farmhouse in the middle of nowhere. Three adults inside. And nary a thought of anything but sex.

It was early evening when they emerged from the guest room. Eleanor had made clear to Dale that her bathroom would be fully available to them, but Marvin was too embarrassed. He pulled his clothes back on and headed for the door. He thanked Eleanor as he departed her house of covert lust, still steeped in the essence of sex.

Dale hung around. She indulged in a leisurely shower and when it came to soaping up her breasts, she allowed her fingers to twirl idly on the nipples much as Marvin had done the day before. She especially enjoyed that.

When Dale was scrubbed and dressed, she joined her friend at the kitchen table.

"Might as well have your dinner here, sweetie," Eleanor offered. "I made stew."

Dale decided to stay for dinner and talk with her friend. It seemed only right, having just enjoyed her ample hospitality. Eleanor was a person of discretion and Dale knew she'd be delicate in asking about the tryst. She'd want to know if Dale felt like talking about it, and if not, there would be no further mention of it.

Dale was undecided. She knew Eleanor would be hungry for details of her sexual encounters. But she also knew it wouldn't be fair to Marvin if she just turned around and gave a blow-by-blow account of things. Neither would it reflect well on her, she was sure.

It was a time for self-assessment. Dale needed to plumb her thoughts and feelings. How much does she owe Marvin? How long will she be sleeping with him? How, after all, does she feel about him?

Dale decided she wouldn't be comfortable talking about the affair just yet, so she steered clear of the subject. But she left no doubt about the obvious, namely that she and Marvin had come to the farmhouse for sex, all the writhing and heavy breathing they could fit into three or four hours.

"I think I figured that out for myself," Eleanor said. "I'll have the place tidied up the next time you come."

Next time!

Dale had been looking to resolve that question, and here it was. *Yes, of course there'll be a next time,* she mused. *There's nothing to lose on such a short term. And besides, I'm having quality sex on a regular basis… for now anyway.*

· · · · · · · · ·

But uncertainty had descended on their affair. Marvin's own conflicts had reached a tipping point. As his timeline with Shannon had grown short, his ardor for Dale had grown hot. He was bent on keeping their liaison alive as long as he could.

Dale felt obliged to lay out this changing scenario to Eleanor. If it was going to continue, that would put greater demands on the farmhouse, to say the least.

Eleanor was typically intrigued by the new developments. She would be happy to host Dale and Marvin's continued meetings there. Their room would be ready.

"Oh, Ellie honey, you're such a dear," Dale said. "I'll straighten up the room. If you could just put out some, uh, fresh sheets that would be great."

Knowing that future bouts with Marvin were now likely to continue a while longer, Dale chuckled to think of the stress that would put on Eleanor's supply of bed linens. She'd have to buy her friend a whole new closet-full simply because both lovers were given to a liberal flow of bodily fluids.

Even at her advanced age, Dale would moisten at the thought of sex. The act of sex would produce a flow. She loved the ample lubrication; it made for smooth and pleasurable intercourse. Most of all, it made her feel young.

Marvin had produced more semen than Dale thought possible. In the few days she'd been with him, he'd shared his plentiful wellspring with her and from there it steadily trickled out of her. It got everywhere on the bed. Based on her own experience, she was quite sure Marvin was exceptional in this regard.

In just a few days, the two of them had made quite a joyful mess of two different beds.

Their present situation, however, was no laughing matter. In very little time Dale had made a deep impression on Marvin. It seemed indelible. She understood that now.

She had entered this relationship with no idea, no plan nor any hope of a plan. But in the course of just a few days she had helped undermine his marriage even before he *got* married. She saw how hard Marvin had fallen for her. She saw his affection for the woman he would marry dwindle away to nothing. And she could see that Marvin was heading for personal disaster.

She blamed herself. She had challenged him to go find a "willing woman" and then she had volunteered to *be* that woman. She had overwhelmed him with her sexual virtuosity and charms, and now he was smitten. She had seduced him.

It was not her first seduction. Dale had discovered her strong seductive powers while still very young. She was strikingly beautiful for all to see, but there was something powerful just under the surface. The enchanting urgency that throbbed in her would leave the few who lay with her utterly transformed. It set her apart from other women.

It was a rare power. But until the right moment came, she kept it to herself, locked away out of sight.

Captivating though she was, she made her way through life as a modest and humble woman. She never let on that, in chosen circumstances, she was a lockbox of potent sexual expression.

Intuitively, she knew the box had been opened for Marvin, and his life would never be the same. Dale believed the man had to be saved. But how? Every possible avenue out of this plight seemed dead-ended as soon as she thought of it. There would be more than a few casualties if Marvin's wedding plans fell apart. Dale could see that many would be hurt, deep resentment would stain their lives, careers could be wrecked. As she pondered this grim outlook, one thing became clear. If Marvin's love for Shannon could be restored, all the other problems would go away.

Dale resolved to tell Marvin these unexpected facts of life. He had been blinded by his irrational response to Dale. He believed he was in love. He needed to see things more clearly.

But she knew it wouldn't be easy. The man's emotional leanings were sharply tilted toward Dale. She understood how hard it would be to simply shift them back to where they'd been.

She knew, in fact, that it would not be possible.

She imagined Marvin and Shannon in their bedroom on her first night back. The scene would be fraught. Problems would show up almost at once. Dale knew next to nothing about Shannon, but she was sure the woman's most ardent ministrations would pale compared to hers.

Marvin had to somehow head off the emotional suicide he was lining up for. He could never strike the last few days from his mind, but he might try to pretend they never happened.

CHAPTER FIVE

The day of Shannon's return arrived. As Marvin and Shannon were driving back from the airport Marvin allowed destructive thoughts to dance freely in his mind.

He couldn't help thinking she was sitting in the very seat Dale sat in on the way to their sexual escapade at the house. He recalled the breathtaking glimpse of ample thigh when she crossed her legs. And he could not reconcile the modest bump in Shannon's blouse that her breasts made, pitifully small by Marvin's new standards.

Piece by piece, Marvin ran a tally of physical features comparing the two women he'd most recently been intimate with. He knew well the corrosive effect of such thinking. But he couldn't stop himself. He'd already begun casting his fiancée out of his thoughts, out of his life.

Shannon meanwhile was showering great affection on her man, as would be expected after five weeks. Marvin did his best, even while driving, to respond but deep inside he was terribly conflicted. He didn't want her. Having tasted Dale's charms, Marvin regarded anything else as a poor copy. There was nothing he could do. He was already in Dale's thrall, and he knew it. All he could do now was continue to pretend.

Once they arrived home, Marvin made a show of returning Shannon's hugs and kisses, but he dreaded the imminent sex. Shannon, none the wiser, was eager to get in bed with Marvin. It had been five weeks.

They got undressed together and Marvin was stunned at how plain and pink and unremarkable Shannon's body was. His perspective had changed radically.

Shannon pulled back the spanking clean powder blue bedspread. As they lay down Shannon noted that Marvin, for the first time in memory, was not rock hard. Things quickly got worse from there.

* * * * * * *

Shannon was supportive of Marvin following his failure in bed. She was marrying the man, she told herself, not the genitals. Besides, it happens to everybody once in a while, or so she'd heard. But Shannon sensed something else missing besides Marvin's awesome erection. He wasn't passionate with her in the way he'd been before her trip. He wasn't emotionally engaged. If Shannon had a suspicious mind, she might have thought all signs pointed to Marvin fooling around while she was gone. But she wasn't given to suspicious thoughts. She made herself believe this blip in their relationship was nothing, not even worth noting in the total scheme.

Marvin, for his part, was desperate for help. He knew his relationship with Shannon was in jeopardy, even though *she* believed things were fine. He feared failure. A broken engagement would bring shock and humiliation. His life and Shannon's would be shipwrecked.

Where could he turn for counsel or support? Instinctively, he wanted to share his concerns with the woman he'd shared his bed with recently.

On its face, turning to Dale for emotional support was madness. It was Dale, after all, who'd led him into so much turmoil in the first place with her enchanting ways. Wasn't she the cause of all this distress? Despite his best try, Marvin could not see Dale as the problem. He could not blame her. He could not think a single negative thought about her. Such was her effect.

"How could you let this happen?" Marvin grumbled out loud.

He was alone in the bedroom, pacing and feverishly mulling the events of the last few days. Shannon meantime had gone out to visit friends, wondering what had become of the man she intended to marry.

"Sure, she propositioned you," he said, recounting the fateful first day. "You could see it was a slip of the tongue. You could've let it pass. You didn't have to take her up on it, right on the spot, and go charging out of the office with her!"

Marvin was fuming. He heaped blame on himself for acting like a reckless teenager and likely ruining his engagement with Shannon. He feared the poor lady would be devastated if he broke it off.

"And where would you be, smart boy?" he said to himself. "You'd be nowhere, and you'd be all by yourself."

Marvin was afraid of being alone. He felt he was about to lose his fiancée. And he could not see his affair with Dale lasting forever either. They couldn't live out their lives meeting at Eleanor's place. There was no future there. What's more, he knew that stringing out the affair with no clear end in sight was unfair to Dale. Their romance was a hard secret to keep. If word of it got out, both of their jobs could be put at risk, to say nothing of his engagement.

If he was ever going to restore the intimacy he shared with Shannon, he knew he had to forget completely the Dale he'd been intensely intimate with in recent days. Forget her beguiling charm and sensuous demeanor. Forget her wondrous brown body that beckoned him beyond his limits.

But that bell could not be un-rung. Marvin knew he could forget about forgetting it. There was no easy fix to his problem. There would be pain. There would be grief. There would be lingering disappointment.

The more Marvin thought about what Dale had done to his life, the more he wanted her. It made no sense at all. Yet in this bewildering moment, seeing Dale again was the only thing on his mind.

* * * * * * *

Dale drove faster than usual to the farmhouse. She knew Marvin was on his way and she didn't want him to get there before she did. She knew he was in an emotional state, and it would be better if Eleanor didn't see that.

Dale expected they'd go right to the guest room to be alone when they arrived. But she couldn't guess what might happen next. Marvin had told her about his failure in bed with Shannon, and he had clumsily linked it to his feelings for Dale.

She had a sense this could be the start of a turbulent new chapter for them.

When she arrived at Eleanor's, she let herself in; she'd long since been given walk-in privileges. Eleanor was sitting in the parlor by the door, mending a pair of shorts.

"Hi, Sweetie. How's your love life?"

"Ellie, I wish I knew. Everything seems to be changing now that Shannon's back."

Dale left out the part about Marvin's impotence. She'd decided not to talk about it till the situation got a little clearer.

"Well, you knew that was coming," Eleanor said. "Frankly, I didn't expect to see you two back here anymore. Looks like you really set the hook in him."

"You're right, but all good things must come to an end," Dale replied.

She believed their affair indeed would soon be ending. Yet uncertainties remained. She also worried that simply cutting the cord on such an intimate connection would lead to frustration, profound frustration for both of them. Dale regretted that she was being less than forthcoming with her longtime confidant. She felt a need to lay it all out for her right now, but she held off. She first needed to know where Marvin's head was. He would be arriving any minute now.

* * * * * * *

It was a different Marvin that accompanied Dale into the guest bedroom. His touch was tentative. He would look searchingly into her eyes, but then look away. They sat on the edge of the bed.

"I had to see you again," Marvin confessed.

"I know," Dale replied. "I think I have an idea of what you're going through."

Marvin was not surprised to hear that. Even in times of tempestuous sex, Dale had shown she was tuned-in to his feelings.

Dale brought her legs up and crossed them on the bed. As she sat there facing Marvin, her white shorts highlighted her abundant thighs. She knew that pose had always been enough to arouse him. It still was. Dale reached for him. They lay together on the bed holding and caressing, their intensity growing. They shared a few kisses as well, something still new for them.

When she thought it was time, Dale whispered, "Don't you think you should take your pants off?"

Marvin was energized. His demeanor and body language shifted back at once to what they'd been in their first days. Dale let out a long breath of relief.

She allowed herself a smug thought, *Nothing wrong with Marvin that a little bit of Dale can't fix.* She knew Marvin was thinking the same thing. Soon they were rolling on the sheets in each other's arms.

We're humping again! Dale thought gleefully. Indeed, the tension they'd both felt earlier was gone. They took generous helpings of each other then. It was a glorious union.

If Eleanor was still listening for sounds coming from the guest room, she was not disappointed.

* * * * * * *

There it was. The situation had been laid out in sharp detail before them. The potency problem that had undermined Marvin's harmony with Shannon—did not exist in the company of Dale. What they both suspected had made Marvin go limp, they now knew. The implications were dire. Marvin agonized over the possible effects of his condition. He again sought out Dale's thoughts on it.

The office layout at NatureSource allowed Marvin and Dale to talk privately, if somewhat guardedly. It made for a bizarre scene. Here were two employees of markedly different ages, dressed for the office, having long talks about life, love and the junction of body and mind. The same two employees who in recent weeks had been romping in energetic sex on the sly.

"I admit it," Marvin said. "I haven't enjoyed the company of a woman like I enjoy you. Not ever, and it's not even close. It's gotten to where I don't think making love to Shannon will ever be possible again. My own fiancée! I couldn't think about anyone but you after our first day at the house. So now here I am looking at my prospects down the road, and they're not good."

The prospects, all of them, were just as grim as he'd been imagining. They dictated that someone would get hurt. Marvin could not function sexually with his fiancée. Shannon's feelings about Marvin were very much in flux. And though it was hard to imagine, Dale didn't figure to remain a world-class lover forever; she was already an older woman by some standards.

Yet at the same time, Dale had come to enjoy the bedroom time with Marvin. It clearly met her definition of quality sex. She'd also begun to feel closer to him personally; she hadn't expected that. She was a phenomenally vital woman in her forties, and life had its rewards. She would be sad to see this affair end.

Still, prudence called for Dale to think more about her own welfare. She couldn't just let events unfold around her with no thought for her future. The resolution must stay in play, she reminded herself.

Nevertheless, she believed most of the big moves yet to come would not be hers.

Chapter Six

Shannon was leaving. Tears ran freely through her eyeshadow, leaving dark circles around her eyes and streaks on her cheeks and neck. She had informed Marvin that she was breaking off the engagement because she felt time was running out on her. Her life plan called for marriage, family and lasting happiness. She never said it, but happiness certainly included a rewarding sex life with her husband. Now she had to start over. She had to begin again searching for the right man to fulfill her dreams. In essence, she was leaving for better sex, but she'd sooner die than say that in so many words, especially to herself.

Even though Marvin favored the break-up, the actual parting with Shannon was emotionally jarring. They'd come too far as a couple not to have emotional investment.

He again sought comfort in Dale, who had become his confidant in these turbulent times, along with her standing as avid sex partner. He found her to be incomparable in each role. They had formed a meaningful bond. The question remaining in both their minds was, how long can this go on? Marvin pictured putting in the years with Dale—whom he still regarded as the world's greatest female—as long as the circumstances were availing. They would not marry though. She would tell him that emphatically. As things presently stood, it would be a very bad look, to say the least.

There were other reasons too. Dale was still emotionally wary in the wake of her previous ill-fated alliances.

She was not unhappy with the new arrangement. But she had no illusions. She too knew the certainties of time, and she was very aware that she was coming up on some tough age brackets even for the world's greatest female. But for now, they were clearly making each other happy.

They sought out each other regularly. They tried to manage now and then without the comfort and security of Eleanor's farmhouse; they wanted to be less frequent visitors. They didn't want to act entitled to their almost daily visits.

But their options were few. Marvin felt shame—or something akin to shame—going back to his own house for their liaisons. The familiarity of it spoke to him of simpler times with Shannon and the plans they'd made. He found it impossibly ill-suited to his present desires. Dale understood completely, though she did miss the powder blue bedspread.

That led them back to Eleanor's place. Eleanor had made her hospitality clear: Her farmhouse was theirs as long as they wanted it. Eleanor had found that creeping close to the door while the couple cavorted inside gave her more stimulation than she could muster on her own. She would slip her hand inside her waistband as she called up her fantasies. It was like standing next to the bed, she thought.

It went on that way for weeks. Dale and Marvin feasted on each other nearly every day, and Eleanor had taken to wearing shorts around the farmhouse.

CHAPTER SEVEN

Marvin and Shannon agreed to put their house up for sale; they were co-owners. The couple wanted to put the failed engagement behind them quickly, so they priced the property to sell. In just four days the house had changed hands.

Marvin and Shannon had no bitterness toward each other. But the nature and pace of many a separation tends to widen the gaps that already exist. They agreed to go to the house separately and remove their personal items. The furniture and fixtures they'd bought together would all go to Shannon, Marvin decided.

Marvin went first because his items were mostly clothing and things he could carry in boxes. He said a silent goodbye to the bed where it all started, where his life had changed irrevocably. It belonged to Shannon now.

Friday, Marvin signed a rental agreement for a townhouse apartment in the nearby town of Bloomfield. From there, NatureSource would be just a twenty-minute drive. Driving to Dale's apartment would take a little longer.

His new townhouse would be ready for him on Monday. He'd have to find a place to stay for three nights. The logical choice, again, was Eleanor's house, their old standby, as she'd continued to offer them unlimited hospitality. That would now include a few overnight stays. She also offered the privacy from neighbors that Dale could not be assured of at her own place.

So with a few items in boxes he'd packed at the house, Marvin accompanied Dale to the guest room at Eleanor's farm. Gabby was staying with her friend for a few days as she had vacated the apartment with Dale.

"Our first home," Marvin quipped.

"I was waiting for you to carry me across the threshold," Dale replied with mock disappointment.

In what amounted to their first time together when they weren't either sitting in the office or having sex, Dale and Marvin went about the everyday functions of bathing and dressing in the limited confines of the guest room and adjoining bath.

Marvin jumped in the shower for a quick wash before changing his clothes. Before that, the only time Dale had seen him naked without an erection was right after sex. Fact is, Marvin's sex organ had always fascinated her. It seemed to respond to her so perfectly, almost like a living creature. Its massive girth had caused her to stretch internally to accommodate it. It was now her personal, custom fitted sex organ.

Thinking about it so intently excited Dale. It made her feel young. On impulse, she pulled off her clothes and presented herself at the shower door. They embraced under the water, and the suddenness of the moment overcame them. Very soon, Dale was gripping the shower railing and Marvin was behind her, clasping her hips as the water pelted them.

It was over in no time. They had a rare facility for satisfying each other completely; that had been clear all along. The two of them stumbled out of the shower and fell face down on the bed. So much for everyday life.

The simple fact was Dale and Marvin couldn't get enough of each other even though they'd already packed a lot of sex into their short time together. Their craving for each other had not slackened at all; it had continued to grow. They both knew how unusual that was. They'd even been kissing in recent weeks, a sure sign their affection was broadening. Things were indeed changing.

They knew the calculus of their relationship didn't work for the long term. At the present time, however, they were content to let nature do its work—for better or worse—in its own time.

CHAPTER EIGHT

Time passed unremarkably. Without fanfare, Dale and Gabby moved-in with Marvin in his sizable townhouse. Gabby took the guest room with bath that was separated from Dale and Marvin by a hallway, affording a high degree of privacy all around.

Dale had come to thrive on the steadiness of their relationship as Marvin fell in comfortably with her life rhythms. They lived much as a contented middle-aged couple might live, save for their energetic brawls between the sheets.

Dale was promoted to a manager position at NatureSource, overseeing a staff of sixteen in consumer relations. When she was briefed on her new responsibilities, she prevailed on the department head to promote Marvin as well, to be her direct report.

They would manage the staff jointly with divided responsibilities. It would be more efficient that way, they all would agree, even though such personnel maneuvers were nearly unheard-of. Their offices abutted each other in a carpeted area at the front of the floor.

Dale and Marvin had made no show of living together, even though such relationships had grown common. But neither had they sought to hide the fact. They both believed the presence of Dale's daughter in the residence only added to the domestic quality of the arrangement.

They did wonder from time to time about how their living arrangement might appear to their employer. Would it be a problem for NatureSource that managers in consumer relations were sharing an apartment? They thought not, but they were hesitant to ask.

Added to those uncertainties, there was the lingering taint of the Shannon episode. An especially nosy person could look at how that went down and how Dale had entered the picture with her co-worker and… safe to say, it still wasn't a good look.

Two years out from the tumultuous afternoon that started their saga, Dale and Marvin observed their second "anniversary" soaking in a hot tub. Their bodies together, the scented suds, the stroking, all invoked the inevitable lust that hovered constantly over them. They made for the bedroom.

As they stood with steaming bodies before the bed, Dale was dumbstruck by what she saw. There in all its luster, a talisman of those poignant times when they first came together—the elegant powder blue bedspread.

Dale was moved by the gesture. It was right in so many ways and it spoke to their growing affinity that it should end up on their own bed after all. Marvin felt justified in spiriting it out of the house. He had seen how well it complemented Dale's alluring coffee color. Dale had noticed the same effect. It made her feel ever more beautiful.

"We'll have to remember to pull it back when we get in bed," Dale said, recalling how mussed and soiled it became in their early days at the house.

Marvin obliged by pulling it back, along with blanket and sheet, but added, "When I'm getting in bed with you, all I can think of is getting in bed with you."

They stood a moment beside the bed, naked from the hot tub and sexually ravenous for each other. They cherished their powerful mutual attraction. They had come to this point in their lives having passed through a portal of events no living person could have predicted. They were happy with each other at this point in their journey, and that was all that mattered. Dale was mindful of her resolution and how far she'd come toward fulfilling it. Her satisfaction was different in kind and degree from any she'd known before.

CHAPTER NINE

Just as crisis appears to slow down the passage of time, living a sedate life makes the weeks and months seem to fly by. In what felt like only a blink, Dale and Marvin now were looking back on four tranquil years since the noise and ferment of secret sex and a ruptured engagement.

Finally, they were able to think about the years ahead. Their relationship, founded entirely on lust, had steadily matured, and one day it came to them they were in love. Their plans for the future began and ended with each other.

They lived quietly together along with Gabby, who pursued her own interests and friends. It was a good arrangement. Dale and Marvin were enjoying each other immensely, savoring life, and not giving much thought to changes down the road. But those changes—unformed, undefined—didn't vanish completely. In Marvin's thinking, they quietly persisted.

He'd been aware that since the beginning of recorded time men and women his age or younger have started families, but he'd kept silent on the matter. He knew Dale was well beyond that age and likely disinclined to raise more children; and he hadn't given any specific thought to the idea himself, especially with Shannon out of the picture. He had a subtle awareness that offspring may never be part of his life. He'd navigated the last few years with a strong desire to keep a really good thing going. Bringing up family concerns could muddy the water with Dale. He was loath to put their present harmony in jeopardy. Marvin believed that life with the world's greatest female was a joy unavailable to other men. It more than compensated for remaining childless, he felt.

But one evening as they lounged on the modest balcony that extended from their bedroom, Dale said, "Ever think about what our children would have been like?"

It was quite out of the blue and it hit Marvin like a dash of cold water. Suddenly his vague back-of-mind notions about children came into sharp focus.

"They'd have been amazing," he said, recovering from his shock. "Just amazing when you think about it."

"They would… they definitely would," Dale said. She sighed dejectedly. "But you know I probably couldn't carry a baby to term," she said, "not at my age. We'd have to find somebody else for that."

"Yeah," Marvin replied somberly. "And who's got the money for *that*?"

In that moment, they became aware that a purely fanciful notion had matured before their eyes as they gave voice to it. Suddenly, having a child was not as abstract as when Dale first said it. It had become a thing. Maybe it was just a matter of money.

"Would you even be willing to *do* that, honey?" Marvin asked, still aware of the matter's highly theoretical nature.

But Dale was way ahead of him. "Who could we get to carry our baby?"

Marvin struggled to keep up with Dale's vaulting thoughts. "They shouldn't be hard to find," he offered. "We're talking about surrogate mothers, right? There must be registries or doctor referrals. It's just that we could never come up with the kind of money they must get. We'd be paying it off the rest of our lives."

"No, I mean somebody we know," Dale went on, "somebody who cares about us. Somebody who'd carry the baby for us."

"That narrows the field a bit, doesn't it!" Marvin chirped. "A young, healthy woman who loves us and is willing to make huge sacrifices for us without asking much in return."

Dale and Marvin grew suddenly still, staring into each other's faces. In that moment their thoughts had converged at the same place—and they both knew it.

"Gabby!"

· · · · · · · · ·

From a factual standpoint, Gabrielle would be a perfect choice for surrogacy. There were many reasons, or so it seemed as Dale and Marvin played out the scenarios. She was twenty-six. She was not romantically involved at present, having in fact been turned off by the procession of fond and clumsy young men who'd tried to woo her. If anyone would settle for less money to carry a baby to term, it might be the daughter. So the thinking went. But Dale and Marvin knew they were trying to wish away the huge and obvious downside to their notion.

"For one thing, Gabby would never go for it," Dale said, falling back onto the hard concrete of everyday.

They sagged at the sudden jolt of reality and fell to mulling their concerns about the Gabby scenario. Their greatest fear was she could grow estranged from her mother for making such an outlandish proposal. Deep inside, they knew the whole idea of a family discount was preposterous. Besides, Gabby would know her prime years for marrying and raising her own kids were not unlimited.

But for the two of them, the thought of bringing a baby into their lives was too enticing to surrender right away. It had a unique lure. It was as if something they'd lost had suddenly been found.

This was their first time as a loving couple that Dale and Marvin had ever spoken about having children. Their circumstances weighed against it. Dale's turn with motherhood had passed many years earlier and her baby had grown up. She had accepted as fact that motherhood was part of her past and her child-bearing role was complete. The fires of her fecundity had all but gone out. But their abrupt notion of a love child had stirred the embers. To her great surprise, Dale was suddenly fascinated.

Marvin too was unexpectedly excited. He had entered their relationship with a clear understanding of Dale's age and all that came with it. But now, with tumbling visions of parenthood dancing in his head for the first time, he felt a peculiar sense of reprieve.

As days went by, Dale and Marvin volleyed their thoughts and fancies of having a baby. As they did, the weight of the Gabby question seemed only to grow heavier. They knew Gabby first had to be introduced to the idea of her mother having a new baby. They expected her to assume the baby would come in the usual way—that Dale would carry it to term. They were all but sure Gabby would raise questions about her mother's limitations for such a task. They felt that might actually prove helpful as an entrée to the topic of surrogacy.

"But what if she just accepts the idea of us having a baby?" Marvin wondered.

"Then we'd have to tell her we're thinking about surrogacy because of my age," Dale replied.

"And," Dale continued, "if Gabby, right then and there, decides she could undertake this burden for her mother—problem solved!"

But Dale and Marvin were not expecting that miracle. They knew better. They were increasingly aware that their thinking had proceeded to such a fanciful level that talking about it to anyone now would not go well.

They had danced around the topic at great length. They kept coming back to the need for Gabby to be part of this family decision. They had no choice. The gravity of the matter was compelling. It threatened an intensely awkward encounter between mother and daughter.

"This is not like proposing a two-week vacation in Barbados," Marvin remarked.

Dale could only agree. "We'll have to be sure she's comfortable with the plan before we can say anything about playing a role," she said. She winced at how casual "playing a role" sounded next to the enormous work the role would involve.

Gabby had remained very close to her mother and continued to live in the same residence with Dale and Marvin. But carrying her mother's fetus? That would be a staggeringly bold departure from the routines they'd known.

On the face of it, the proposal would be so unexpected, so extraordinary, so outré that Dale could not imagine it happening. She even had twinges of fear that Gabrielle might think her mother had lost her mind. But even if Gabby did agree to carry the baby, and to receive a sharply reduced fee, it would amount to Dale asking her daughter to do something for just-so-much that other women would only do for so much more. She had foreboding about that. She feared it could weaken her bond with Gabby. And even then, Dale knew she still would struggle to pay it.

But all their plotting and agonizing would come to nothing if they didn't act. They would have to go where the facts led them. They could begin with the near-certainty that Dale would need fertility therapy at the outset.

"It's not like I keep getting pregnant these days," she remarked. "We've had how many opportunities?

They chuckled at the irony: A relationship founded on sexual intercourse not resulting in a single pregnancy.

They both knew pregnancy for Dale was not only hard to achieve—but also risky. There were greater dangers of birth defects for the child, and complications for the mother.

All the grim certainties, as well as the imponderables, left them with only one workable course: fertility therapy for Dale in order to conceive, followed by a surrogate pregnancy with Gabby. And a lot of luck.

But Gabby had not agreed to the plan; in fact, she knew nothing of it. That would have to be the first thing to change.

As Monday proceeded to Thursday, Dale and Marvin's on-and-off discussions took a subtle turn. Without knowing anything specific about genetic similarities between mother and daughter, they had formed in their minds a notion that a mother/daughter surrogacy would have unique advantages. It was a tantalizing notion for aspiring parents, even knowing they could not find any documented proof of its validity.

Without doubt, Gabby had distinct similarities to her mother. She had the same brown eyes and she'd shocked Marvin once or twice by assuming facial expressions identical to her mother's.

She had the same body as the younger Dale, though her skin was slightly lighter. Marvin time and again would suppress fantasies brought on by the sight of a younger version of his lover. He imagined that some of Dale's most alluring qualities were also shared by Gabby. These thoughts remained intensely private, however. They were not for sharing.

· · · · · · · ·

The day of revelation came. Dale and Marvin sat in their small living room where they waited for Gabby. Dale had asked her to join them there for a "family discussion".

Dale wondered what Gabby could possibly think it was all about. She had never asked her daughter to meet with her anywhere simply to talk. Their relationship was much closer than that. She hoped that Marvin's presence would help explain the difference.

Dale was on edge. She feared she was flirting with estrangement from her daughter. Yet at the same time she could not dismiss the urge just to get it all out at once: "Gabby honey, how about going with us to a fertility clinic where they take our embryo and implant it in your uterus so you can carry it for nine months and give birth to our baby? Your sibling! Does that sound like something you might be willing to do? I'd pay you of course."

But Dale never said that, or anything remotely like it. She didn't have to. It was almost shocking to Dale and Marvin just how much Gabby already knew, or at least surmised, about their relationship.

They talked through the general parts of their quest, as Dale had come to call it. She'd stopped calling it a plan because it was too uncertain, too incomplete to be a plan. And besides, it seemed to suggest scheming.

In the end, Gabby showed greater maturity than she'd ever displayed to Dale or Marvin. She suggested they have a medical consultation together to learn about procedures, roles, risks, timelines, costs—and expectations. Then they could make a better decision.

It was the wise course to take, and Dale and Marvin knew it. They were both a little stunned that Gabby had cut through all their confusion, all their doubts, all their irresolution, with such ease. They had agreed to nothing but consulting with doctors and counselors, yet it came as a clarifying stroke of insight. It was also subtly evident that Gabby had not said no to surrogacy. For the moment, however, it seemed their course was so much clearer now than it had been an hour before.

Chapter Ten

Guidance from doctors and counselors was far from hopeful.

In a round of physical exams and social counseling by a panel of fertility experts from Johnson Community Hospital, along with consultants who specialized in surrogacy cases, Dale and Marvin and Gabby got a step-by-step breakdown of what happens before, during, and after an embryo is transferred to a surrogate mother. The process left them numb and dispirited.

The fertilization, they learned, almost always takes place in a lab where the woman's best eggs are mated up with the man's best sperm and then are cultured there for a few days. The best of those, the one deemed most likely to survive, would become an embryo for insertion through a tube into the uterus of the woman who would carry the baby.

For Dale and Marvin, the bleakest part was the complete absence of sex in the process. No hot embraces, no cries of passion, no joyous moment of conception. The whole procedure was impersonal and clinical in the extreme. It was nothing like they'd imagined. The heady notion of a love child was dashed from their minds. They must turn instead to the lab, the petri dish, the three- or four-day wait for fertilization. For Dale and Marvin this was a kick in the gut.

Then the *coup de grace*: Dale's personal medical history had presented a disturbing profile. Her advanced age had left her only marginally fertile. Worse, her heavy regimen of antidepressants following the breakup of her marriage gave the doctors pause. They feared she faced a higher risk of producing an ill-formed embryo, portending serious defects. It would be their firm admonition not to proceed.

As the panel filed into the conference room, Maurice Silverman, M.D., head of obstetrics at Johnson Community Hospital, and leader of the surrogacy panel, motioned for Marvin to step aside for a moment.

"I wanted to talk to you privately before I go over our findings with you and your partner," he said. "Sadly, your chances for a perfectly healthy baby are virtually nil. We would advise *against* embryo transfer or any pregnancy. Your partner, Dale, presents a disturbing profile for severe complications." Silverman leaned closer to Marvin and lowered his voice. "You have a better chance of getting the child you want if you just directly impregnate the daughter, Gabrielle." He paused, searching Marvin's face for reaction. Then, hastily, he added, "But clearly that's not done in our society, and I'm ethically constrained from even mentioning it."

Marvin was dumbstruck. He was unable to process what he'd just heard.

Finally, he sputtered "Are you suggesting I just hop in the sack with Dale's daughter and hope the genetics pan out?"

"Certainly not, as I just plainly emphasized!" Silverman retorted testily, though still keeping his voice low. "My comment to you was private and off the record. I never said it."

"Doctor Silverman," Marvin persisted, gasping for breath, "there's no way that could ever happen with us. Why, even mentioning it to the women…"

"Of *course* there's no way it could happen," the doctor broke in. His black and silver hair shook with this flash of anger. "I thought I made that clear to you."

Had Dr. Silverman imagined for a moment that he was not a physician with an oath of healing and bound by the ethos of Western civilization? Had he indulged a barbaric non-medical fantasy within a medical situation? If so, his thoughts were hatched deep inside his own imagination and were, to say the least, highly unusual. And profoundly unprofessional. The doctor had planted the thought of Marvin copulating with Gabrielle. As soon as he gave voice to it, he strenuously wished he hadn't. He wanted to see it quickly and entirely forgotten. And he wished Marvin would just drop it.

For the moment, Marvin did. He gathered himself, stood off from the group awhile, exhaled deeply, and then walked to his seat next to Dale at the table. Silverman took his place at the head of the table as though nothing had transpired between him and Marvin just moments before.

But Marvin's imagination was a running jumble of wild notions and primitive passions.

• • • • • • • • •

Dale knew nothing about Dr. Silverman's churlish remarks to Marvin. She sat with him as the panel of experts intoned their judgments. They gave a faint glimmer of hope by suggesting that fertility treatments might boost Dale's prospects slightly, but they were clear that chances for significant change were scant. The medical risks were too great.

As they drove home, Dale fought back her disappointment. The doctors had been signaling for nearly two days that her problems were likely too great to overcome. Now that their decision was clear, she was deflated but not shocked.

Marvin, for his part, said very little during the drive. He was privately wondering whether to tell Dale about Silverman at some point. Every sensible voice in his head said no, just let it pass.

Gabby sat in the back seat peering out the window, oblivious to the Silverman proposal and Marvin's burgeoning interest in it.

There was an impish voice inside Marvin that wanted to stay with the proposal a little longer. Marvin was familiar with this voice. It was his inner psyche, seeking only pleasure no matter how bizarre. He knew the Silverman idea called for an atrocious act completely apart from civilized norms. It would have to be done in strict secrecy and only with the willing collaboration of Dale and Gabby. It would of course never, ever happen.

Marvin was left to mull the matter privately. He pictured Gabby in sheer blue lace opening her bedroom door for him, letting him in. He imagined her touching his arm as he entered, pressing the door closed and turning to him.

Marvin pounded his fist on his leg to cut the revery short. He knew it would be toxic to his relationship with Dale. Nothing good could ever come of it. That genie must never get out of the bottle.

CHAPTER ELEVEN

Dale needed to meet with Dr. Silverman to go over her fertility regimen. It would be a last-ditch measure. Marvin accompanied her. To Marvin, the doctor was not a highly regarded obstetrician so much as a wild-eyed wizard of barbaric practices. He had, intentionally or not, awakened in Marvin a raging lust that churned in the privacy of his imagination.

While Dale was getting dressed Marvin stood alone with Dr. Silverman. Marvin was still agitated by their encounter the day before, and Silverman could see it.

"I was *not* suggesting you have intercourse with the daughter," he said sternly. Silverman had been reading Marvin's thoughts. "If she were involved," he continued, "you would use the same in-vitro process we use for most pregnancies here. It's just that the mother must initiate it. We are professionally barred from advocating it."

"What mother must initiate what?" Marvin wondered.

He was supremely perplexed. His head swirled with jumbled notions of mothers and fathers and babies. It seemed Silverman was *still leaving open* the possibility of Gabrielle carrying her own child—fathered by Marvin. But why? Why would Silverman do that? Was he aware of Marvin's private attraction to Gabby? Was he tormenting Marvin for his own amusement? If so, he was effectively doing it outside the attention of others. Nobody knew about his words with Marvin. Marvin had again allowed Silverman to dumbfound and frustrate him. He believed the doctor had woven a fictional narrative into the facts of their case and had presented it to Marvin privately. It was, Marvin thought, a tempered version of his original "directly impregnate" comment. Marvin came to believe that Silverman was acting out a fantasy of his own about the fair Gabrielle. Why else, he wondered, would Silverman call him aside to talk privately?

But Silverman had previously denied any such intention, and he would certainly do so again. That would have to be that. Marvin fumed at the situation and his puerile reactions. He had let himself be swept away by Silverman's salacious fantasy to the point where he could not see what was in plain sight.

"Yes, of course," he said to Silverman. He could never admit that Silverman had led him astray and that he'd completely lost sight of the medical process.

Nothing more was said about it. The matter that had existed between the two of them, simply ended. Nobody else knew about it, and nobody ever would.

· · · · · · · · ·

But Marvin needed to attend to his thoughts and emotions. He self-assessed his actions of recent days, assembling the pieces that had nearly led to disaster. He'd yielded to a wild notion of procreation for the sake of... the sake of what?

The answer, the truth, shocked him. But it did not surprise him. He knew that what he'd heard, and thought he heard, from Silverman was colored by his undeniable lust for Gabby.

That was the sum and substance of it.

He'd lived in the same house with her as she blossomed into a beautiful young woman. In that time Marvin had been intrigued by Gabby, then fascinated, until finally he saw that he was seriously attracted to her. He wanted her.

Marvin now understood the frustrations of young men everywhere for all time who've lusted for a woman they know they'll never have. Yet there in the medical center a doctor had unveiled a way Marvin could realize his fantasies. Or so he chose to believe.

From there and for a short while, Marvin had effectively lost his mind. He'd ignored the clear denials and the medical impossibility that any such process could happen. He'd set aside the certainty that Gabby and Dale would be perfectly *horrified* at the thought of his fathering a child with Gabby. And he was frighteningly aware that it would not have produced a "close copy" of Dale's baby at all. It would have been his and Gabby's baby.

It was a reckless fantasy. Later, when his good sense had come back to him, Marvin saw that his private words with Silverman still distressed him. He believed the doctor had a strange fondness for titillation by proxy.

"How could I not see that?" Marvin wondered. "What happened to me?"

On reflection, Marvin saw clearly what had happened to him. He had been inordinately swayed by one word—"impregnate". That word had always called up the most basic act of sexual union. No petri dishes or uterine tubes, no lab coats, no waiting around. Just basic organic sex on rumpled sheets with bedcovers hurled aside. To Marvin it was an immensely powerful word, not unlike "humping" had been years before. Its power had led him, in his mind, to the bed down the hall where Gabrielle waited for him.

· · · · · · · ·

In the short time of Marvin's private rapture, Dale seemed to recede into her own thoughts and feelings. That's how it appeared to Marvin at least. Perhaps it was just as well, he thought, lest he appear indifferent to her charms.

But once the medical consultation was over and their lives had returned to a familiar pace, Marvin re-woke to a central truth in his life: Dale was still a stunningly beautiful and charming woman—just as he'd always known her to be. She was still the world's greatest female.

He regretted his bizarre fancies of Gabrielle and the distraction they'd caused. Deep inside he was immensely thankful that neither Gabby nor Dale was ever aware of that episode.

He knew he'd deflected a bullet to the heart of his relationship.

Chapter Twelve

Dale was half-hearted in following through with her fertility therapy. She had no illusions about it. She didn't believe it would change anything for her and she suspected Dr. Silverman had recommended it just to soften the blow of the panel's dire tidings. Eventually she told him she didn't want to pursue it any further.

By now, however, Dr. Silverman had become Dale's *de facto* gynecologist. Since Bogie left her, Dale had paid no heed to the routine exams, tests, and screenings associated with reproductive and sexual health. Silverman had discovered these neglected areas while looking at her records. She was seeing him now strictly to close that gap.

Marvin was uneasy with this arrangement. He was sure when Dale dropped the fertility therapy that Silverman had finally and forever passed into history. Marvin's brush with the doctor was his alone to live with. Dale knew nothing of it, and Marvin had decided she never would.

Now, however, with Silverman playing even a small role in Dale's care, Marvin chafed at the possibilities. He was not comfortable with the man.

Professionally, Silverman had impeccable credentials. Though he was known at times to be pompous and overbearing with colleagues and patients alike, he was highly respected in the ob-gyn community, and an authority in the field of female fertility.

But Marvin had seen a different side. He was sure he had glimpsed a perverse facet of the man lurking beneath the spotless reputation. He didn't trust him. And he was privately incensed that Silverman had access to Dale's body.

CHAPTER THIRTEEN

In what would be her last Silverman appointment for a while, Dale reported to the reception area and took a seat. Two other patients sat waiting as well. It was common for Silverman to see three or four patients at once in separate treatment rooms.

Dale sat next to a younger woman who was completing a patient profile for the office records.

"That profile is so annoying," she commented casually. "It's like there's nothing private anymore."

"Oh, I don't mind really," the woman replied. "They're going to find out whatever they want anyway."

Dale was startled. She'd heard that voice before. As they continued chatting, the woman confided that she was seeing Silverman because she'd miscarried twice. She was plainly distressed.

Why is she telling me this? Dale wondered. *Who talks about their miscarriage in the waiting room?*

"Ms. Blackman, you can complete the form after your appointment, if need be," the receptionist called out cheerfully.

Dale froze. The name was permanently etched on her brain. *Is this the Blackman who destroyed my life five years ago?* she asked herself. Dale was sure it was. She was sitting next to Kristine Blackman.

The woman looked to be in her late twenties, dark, mixed race, straight black hair that touched her shoulders and glistened in the soft light of the waiting room. She was a bit taller than Dale, lean and toned. Dale imagined her writhing in bed with Bogie. She saw Kristine's thighs wrapping around Bogie's naked body. She saw them coupling urgently. She imagined their passion. Dale clenched her fists, struggling to keep a lid on her turbulent feelings.

Don't let her know, screamed her inner voice, *don't give it all away!*

They sat a few moments in silence as Dale collected herself.

Finally, she offered, "It must be incredibly hard to lose a baby."

Kristine nodded slightly in reply. "Yes," she whispered. "Yes, it is."

She fell silent again.

A moment or two passed as Dale mulled her next words. She knew this would be her only chance to say anything to the woman who'd rudely altered her life. She was also aware that, to her mind, charity has no room for vengeance. Conflicting emotions tore at her. Finally, she settled on a middle course.

"Well, when you lose something important, you have to learn to move on. That's just the way it is."

It was not a harmless comment; it was meant to have an edge. She knew she'd run out of ways to get anything more out of Kristine without revealing herself. Their karmic encounter would come to an end there in Dr. Silverman's waiting room.

As she reflected on their brief exchange, however, Dale came to see there wasn't a lot more to learn about Kristine Blackman. Nothing she really needed to know. She knew intuitively that Kristine, with her sleek and youthful features, would appeal to most men, including Bogie by all appearances. But she also knew that it wasn't Kristine's good looks and sex appeal that made Bogie bolt. There had to be another reason.

When it came to relations with men, Dale had never felt inferior to any other women. As the years passed and lovers came and went, Dale knew at her deepest level that she gave them everything they'd ever hoped for—and much more. She was attentive and kind and caring. She was affectionate, often passionate, and bewilderingly beautiful. And in the minds of every one of them, she was incomparable between the sheets.

Why then, she wondered, did Bogie leave her? Why did this keep happening?

Despite these questions and disturbing doubts, Dale was increasingly confident that things had changed since she forged her resolution. She was still very happy with Marvin, even with his furtive eye for other women. She had come to believe they would live out the years together.

Or would Marvin be the next to leave her?

She had no reason to believe he would. But neither had she any reason with the other men who'd left her over the years. And that certainly included Bogie. Dale understood that if Marvin should then leave her after all their emotional adventures together, she would be destitute of hope. She was too invested in their relationship. Her life would turn gravely for the worse.

This tenuous thought lived quietly in a tiny place in the back of her mind.

CHAPTER FOURTEEN

On the surface, life for the three of them proceeded as they'd come to expect. Dale and Marvin followed their careers at NatureSource. Employment at a public utility is not famous for its excitement. It gave stability to their lives, and steady income.

Their very first encounter there—which led to epic sex in Marvin's bedroom—was of course the singular exception to the steadiness and occasional tedium of their jobs.

"No way anybody ever tops that," Marvin crowed one day when the two of them were talking about their workplace. "NatureSource could never put *that* in a promotional brochure."

Indeed, six years out, they seemed to have made a clean break from the affair. There had been no fallout from Marvin's broken engagement, and the subsequent emergence of Dale as a partner. In fact, the only person who truly knew what had happened was Eleanor, and Eleanor by nature kept her own counsel.

Gabby continued to live with them while she pursued a degree in business and then began a career as a financial advisor. She did most of her work from home and had outfitted a room in the house as an office and studio where she conducted online meetings. Business was good; she had planned well. She still had her bed and bath upstairs, down the hall from Dale and Marvin. That was still a lingering a problem.

Dale was always comfortable living with Gabby, as she had for most of Gabby's life. But when they moved into Marvin's townhouse, things changed. The tranquil atmosphere they'd made for themselves became charged when a man was added to the mix.

The room at the end of the hall was the place where Gabby dressed and bathed and slept. It was nearly a perfect setting for Marvin's fervid imagination. Glimpses here and there, the occasional door left open, all gave substance to his fantasies. Indeed, if there was any threat to Dale and Marvin's relationship, it might have been his secret lust for Gabrielle. It had been his private obsession ever since she moved in. He was extremely chary in hiding it from the world. He knew it was radioactive.

What he didn't know was how much Gabby was already aware of his lascivious thoughts. He wasn't fooling her at all, and he wasn't fooling Dale either.

Dale believed that Marvin would never act on his fantasies, and as such his wandering eye would not be a problem. But it troubled her deeply that his fantasies had recently focused on her beloved daughter. It was an unspoken worriment for the women of the house. But what was to be done about it?

. . . .

One day while Dale was out shopping, Marvin was toweling off after a shower. As he pulled up his boxers, there was a single knock on the bedroom door, the perfunctory kind of rap that unbidden visitors make as they're coming in.

Marvin stood in his shorts, gaping at the door in wonderment. He knew Dale was not home. The only other person in the house was Gabby.

. . . .

Gabrielle stepped inside and closed the door behind her. She wore a brown bathrobe with white piping, and apparently nothing else. She was looking directly into Marvin's eyes but her face betrayed no intention. He felt a surge in his gut; he knew his life was about to change. Gabby walked slowly toward him; her eyes still fixed on his. When she got close enough to touch, she stopped. Marvin felt her bodily presence.

In these fleeting moments, Marvin could not think clearly, could not speak. He could not act rationally at all. Instead, with the object of his lustful desires standing and breathing just inches away, all he could do was spring an erection that threatened to poke a hole in his shorts.

A silence closed in on them as they faced each other. Finally, Gabrielle spoke.

"You see what you're doing?" she hissed. "You are dishonoring my mother. She is the most wonderful woman you could ever hope to meet. She loves you without reservation. She expects nothing in return but your unqualified love.

But what do you do to show your devotion?" Gabrielle continued, her anger rising. "You turn your head to ogle other women wherever you are, even when you're with her. You look at their bodies, you size them up. And worst of all, Marvin, you look at me! You look at me every chance you get. You want me! You want my body!" Gabrielle was spitting the words now. "You can't keep a good thing going," she continued. "You have a perfect partner in your life, and yet you're always on the hunt for something new, even something forbidden. And that's what I am, Marvin—I'm forbidden!"

With that, Gabrielle launched a powerful open-hand swing, arcing from her knees like a cane cutter with his bolo, whacking Marvin's bulging phallus barely covered by his shorts.

Marvin shuddered and nearly lost his balance. He winced at the stinging pain but kept silent.

"That thing's going to get you in real trouble someday," she cried. "And you'll regret it for the rest of your life. The sooner you see that, the better it'll be for all of us."

She turned and strode briskly to the door, opened it, then turned back to Marvin and cast a glare at the shriveling member in his shorts. Her eyes met Marvin's a last time, anger flushing her face. Then she turned and walked out, closing the door firmly behind her.

· · · · · · · · ·

Marvin had suffered a staggering blow to his male ego. But he now saw he had it coming. The incident with Gabby had done more than leave a welt on his private parts. It made him reflect on his behavior. He had glimpsed himself as Gabby had seen him. He knew the truth in her admonition, "You'll regret it for the rest of your life." Marvin now saw that his furtive glances at women were not furtive at all. The women knew. But Marvin had been unaware that they knew—until Gabby had jarringly made that clear.

He had debased himself. He felt humiliated, realizing he may now have a reputation as a cheap philanderer. And worse by far was how he must have looked to Dale all along. It grieved Marvin to imagine how Dale had steadfastly kept any pain to herself. How could he make it up to her?

He knew it wasn't possible. The only hope left to him would be to focus all his loving energies on her, make her know how much he valued her, and maintain that intensity every single day. He hoped he had dodged another bullet. He vowed it would be the absolute last.

Chapter Fifteen

Dale knew nothing about the Gabby confrontation. By coincidence, she had begun a more intense focus on her relationship with Marvin. She was reacting to fears that he could be the next lover to jump ship without the slightest warning or indication.

The question of why men in her life, including her ex-husband and most recently Bogie, saw fit to cheat on her remained unanswered. She'd pondered every possible cause she could think of, but she knew nothing could be proved. The question that had perplexed her throughout most of her adult life would remain a mystery.

But it would not remain a problem. She had no further interest in it. She had finally moved past it. She believed she and Marvin together had turned a vital corner in their lives. They were both more focused on each other, no longer distracted by people and events of their past.. They were determined to make their lives a celebration of their unique bond. They knew their affinity had grown well beyond the bedroom into true love. It had more promise of lifelong happiness than either had ever known. They understood its oddly inverted nature. It was contrary to the time-honored ways of life and love. But there it was.

Dale and Marvin had made an unspoken commitment to each other. For life.

CHAPTER SIXTEEN

One night after pulling back the powder blue bedspread, the couple shared a goodnight kiss that surpassed all others. It was born of a conviction—arrived at separately but shared together—that all remaining discord, all the threats to their love had finally been put to rest. They slept peacefully.

Dale dreamed of an unusual gathering in a grassy field like the pasture outside Eleanor's farmhouse. She was there to see, as was Eleanor, but not to be seen. Dale's prized powder blue bedspread was draped over the top rail of the fence bordering the pasture. It seemed only natural that it should be there. She thought she knew all the people assembled there but could not name them. They seemed bewildered, not knowing one another, nor where they were, or why.

Then, as if on a signal, they began to file out of the pasture through the gateway where Dale was standing. She was close enough to see their faces. But they all seemed to be strangers at first, following other strangers.

After a while, Dale began to recognize them. Shannon Pierce walked by, darting her head this way and that, like a bird searching for something. More strangers plodded past before Kristine Blackman appeared, looking lithe and hungry like a predator. She was followed closely by Bogie, and they appeared to be arguing heatedly. Again more faces went by. Dale was aware that some of them were the nosy neighbors from her apartment years.

The last of the bunch was Dr. Silverman, his hair more silver than Dale remembered. He was waving an arm and seemed to be shouting instructions. But they had their backs to him and were not listening.

When everyone had passed out of the pasture, Eleanor swung the gate shut and hooked it in place. Leaning back cross-legged against the fence, she beamed at Dale as she had for years when she got to the end of a story she was telling, and love had prevailed over duress.

"Well, we won't be seeing *them* anymore," she said.